SOME
BUGS

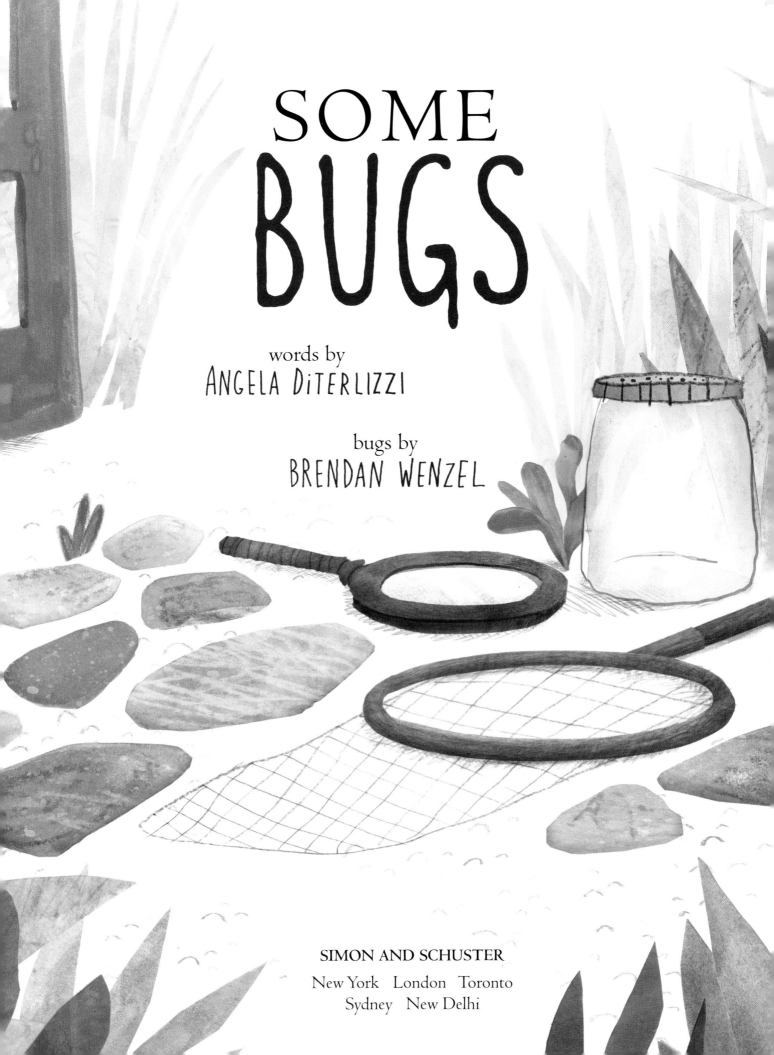

SOME
BUGS

words by
ANGELA DiTERLIZZI

bugs by
BRENDAN WENZEL

SIMON AND SCHUSTER

New York   London   Toronto
Sydney   New Delhi

Some bugs
STING.

Some bugs
BITE.

Some bugs
STINK.

And some bugs

FIGHT!

Some bugs
FLUTTER.

Some bugs
CRAWL.

Some bugs
curl up in a
BALL.

Some bugs
HOP.

Some bugs
GLIDE.

Some bugs
SWIM.

And
some bugs
HIDE!

Some bugs
CLICK.

Some bugs
SING.

Some bugs do a
BUZZING
thing!

Some bugs
BUILD.

Some bugs
HUNT.

Some bugs
MAKE.

And some bugs
TAKE!

STINGING, BITING,
STINKING, FIGHTING,
HOPPING, GLIDING,
SWIMMING, HIDING.

BUILDING, MAKING,
HUNTING, TAKING—
bugs are oh-so-
FASCINATING!

So
KNEEL
down close,

LOOK
very hard,

and find
SOME BUGS
in your backyard!

For T. and my little bug, Soph, who love all things tiny
—A. D.

For those who encouraged me to play outside
— B. W.

SIMON AND SCHUSTER

First published in Great Britain in 2014 by Simon and Schuster UK Ltd, 1st Floor, 222 Gray's Inn Road, London, WC1X 8HB. A CBS Company •
Originally published in 2014 by Beach Lane Books, an imprint of Simon and Schuster Children's Publishing Division, New York • Text Copyright © 2014
by Angela DiTerlizzi. Illustrations Copyright © 2014 by Brendan Wenzel. All rights reserved. • The right of Angela DiTerlizzi and Brendan Wenzel to be
identified as the author and illustrator of this work has been asserted by them in accordance with the Copyright, Designs and Patents Act, 1988 • All rights
reserved, including the right of reproduction in whole or in part in any form • A CIP catalogue record for this book is available from the British Library upon
request • ISBN: 978-1-4711-2173-9 (PB) • Printed in China • 10 9 8 7 6 5 4 3 2 1 • www.simonandschuster.co.uk

Special thanks to Brendan Wenzel
for creating the perfect backyard microcosmos
and to Andrea, Allyn, and Lauren for giving this book wings —A. D.